P9-DSY-256

The Ḥanukkah of Great-Uncle Otto

The Ḥanukkah of

Great-Uncle Otto

Myron Levoy

illustrated by
DONNA RUFF

The Jewish Publication Society of America
Philadelphia 5745/ 1984

Copyright © 1984 by Myron Levoy
Printed in the United States of America

Library of Congress Cataloging in Publication Data
Levoy, Myron.

  The Hanukkah of great-uncle Otto.

  Summary: Joshua and his great-uncle Otto discover
a new meaning in the celebration of Hanukkah when they
try to build a menorah like a special one Otto lost
during the Holocaust.
  1. Children's stories, American. [1. Hanukkah—
Fiction. 2. Uncles—Fiction] I. Ruff, Donna, ill.
II. Title.
PZ7.L5825Han 1984   [Fic]   84-12635
ISBN 0-8276-0242-1

Designed by Adrianne Onderdonk Dudden

For Oscar,
an uncle who is great

JOSHUA KNEW that Ḥanukkah was coming. The holiday was in the bare trees, their few remaining leaves shaking like candle flames. It was in the first thin snow, covering the ground like fine lace. But most of all, it was in his Great-Uncle Otto.

"Joshua," Great-Uncle Otto said in his booming voice of old Europe, "Ḥanukkah is flying toward us like a winter bird, a bird with shining wings spread like a great candelabrum. I can hear it from far off just as I did when I was a little boy in Europe, in Germany. The same winter bird—Ḥanukkah."

As he spoke, Great-Uncle Otto reached for the tea kettle,

but slowly, for his arms were crippled with arthritis and his hands were as stiff as the frozen earth. Seeing him struggle, Joshua leaped up and put the battered kettle on the hot plate. And since his great-uncle always liked something sweet with his tea, Joshua searched in a drawer of the big oak desk for the bag of halvah.

Around them in the shop was the clutter of many years: copper pipes like streaks of lightning, wood in strips and blocks, cast-iron machinery too heavy to move and all the old ovens, refrigerators, lawn mowers, chairs, and tables that customers had left for repairs and had never taken back. Joshua and his friends had often used this great jungle of discarded wreckage for imaginary space missions and undersea battles. And at the end of their games, there was always something for them: paper cups with soda or milk or juice. Uncle Otto always had paper cups for everyone—the children, the customers, the mail carrier, the rent.collector, everyone.

But now there were no more customers, for Great-Uncle Otto could no longer hold the repair tools in his stiff, trembling hands. He couldn't even hold his cup without spilling tea all

over the desk. So he let Joshua help him with his tea every afternoon, but only when they were alone.

At home, Uncle Otto dropped food at the table and wouldn't let anyone help him. He would tell Joshua's mother, "I'm not a cripple! I'm not a baby!"

"He's too proud, that's what he is," Joshua's mother would say when Otto wasn't there. "Too proud to let anyone do anything for him."

At home, Uncle Otto was an old man, a sad, quiet man, and not a great-uncle at all.

But in his shop, in his chair by the desk, he could still be a tower of strength, a teller of stories, a great-uncle wiser than any book. And so he went to his shop each day, saying, "In case a customer comes, I can still repair anything." But Joshua knew that Great-Uncle Otto really went to his shop to become himself again.

Uncle Otto waved his arm slowly and said, "Hanukkah is beating its wings nearer and nearer. Yes, it is." Joshua watched his thin white hair float above his head as he nodded again and again. "Hanukkah is almost here."

"Uncle Otto? Could you tell me a Ḥanukkah story?"
asked Joshua. "A real long one?"

"I'll tell you a short one," said Uncle Otto, "but a true
one. It happened—let me see—seventy-five years ago across
the ocean in Germany, when times were happy, long before
Hitler came with his ugly, lunatic hate. I was a little boy then,
as young as you, Joshua. It was the first night of Ḥanukkah—
wait! the hot plate is on too high; the teapot will burst—the first
night, and I was supposed to put the menorah on the table and
light the *shammes,* the center candle, just as you do now. Ah,
that menorah. It was old even then. It was my father's father's
menorah. Imagine!"

As he lowered the heat under the teapot, Joshua said, "It
must be two-hundred years old by now."

"At least," his great-uncle said. "So I took the menorah
and—who could believe it—I dropped it. It slipped, I tripped,
who knows. The delicate arms were bent out of shape, and I
stood there crying because I was afraid of what my father
would do. Fathers then weren't like fathers now. They were
strict. Serious. Stern. They loved us—oh, yes—but with a strict,

serious, stern love. So there I was, scared as if I had burned down the house. And what did my father do? Did he hit me with a belt? Did he?"

"Yes!" said Joshua decisively.

"He didn't!" Great-Uncle Otto boomed. "Strict, serious, stern, but he didn't. No. He took the menorah and bent the arms this way, that way, and little by little they were almost straight. And he asked me why I was crying like a broken ḥalil, like a broken reed flute. The menorah was damaged, yes. But that wasn't so important. The *meaning* of the menorah, that was important. That was valuable. And that could never be damaged. And my father asked me, while I was still shaking, what I thought the menorah meant. So I'll ask you. What do you think?"

Joshua hesitated, just as he did in school, afraid of making a mistake and looking foolish. In class, he always sat quietly, never answering if he could help it. "The quiet one," his mother called him.

"It's . . . it's about the Jewish people," said Joshua, "and how they fought to get their temple back from the enemy, King

Antiochus. And when they won, they lit the menorah in the temple. There was only enough oil for one day, but it burned for eight days, and that's why we light one candle on the first night of Hanukkah, and two candles on the second night, and so on, up to eight. But you know, I wish we could light all eight candles every night.''

"Ah!" said Great-Uncle Otto. "But that's it! One candle, then two, then three. That's where the real meaning hides, my father said. The menorah tells us how freedom spreads, how faith spreads, how kindness spreads. The servant candle in the center of the menorah—the *shammes*, the ''sexton''—gives its light to another candle and another, until that one little light becomes many lights, becomes a beacon, a festival, a feast of lights. That's what my father said to me, and that's what can never be lost or damaged, no matter what happens to the menorah. For me, this memory has become a true part of the Hanukkah story. Yes. Yes. We all have our special memories. Someday you'll have yours, too. And the teapot's boiling over!''

As Joshua raised the kettle off the hot plate and prepared

a cup of tea, he wondered what special memory he would ever have about Hanukkah. He carefully raised the cup to Great-Uncle Otto's lips, and Otto put his shaking hands over Joshua's hands as if he, too, were holding the cup.

"Ahh, that's good hot tea," said Great-Uncle Otto, "prepared by my expert." He took a long sip, then a nibble of hal-

vah, and gave a deep sigh. After a moment he said, "Ḥanukkah is coming, yes, and this beautiful holiday should be happy. But not for me. No. No. I'm completely useless now. Your mother and father have to help me with everything." He pushed back his chair abruptly and stared out the window at the snow. There was a long moment of silence.

Joshua tried to think of something cheerful to say. Great-Uncle Otto had never been like this in his shop before. Maybe at home, but not here. He remembered how his great-uncle had cheered *him* up last year when his dog, Feller, had finally died of old age. But now Uncle Otto seemed just as old and sad and helpless as Feller had been.

"Uncle Otto," Joshua said softly, trying to tiptoe around the edge of his sadness, "you aren't useless at all. You can do all kinds of things. If you want, you can help me light the *shammes* for Ḥanukkah." He carefully lifted the teacup again.

"Ummm," Uncle Otto murmured, pushing the cup aside. He stared out the window once more.

"You can light *all* the candles," said Joshua, trying harder to cheer him up. "Dad wouldn't mind. Okay?"

"Aha, Joshua," Great-Uncle Otto said sadly. "That's exactly it. Your father wouldn't mind this. Your mother wouldn't mind that. I do nothing for them anymore. Nothing. They feed me. They clothe me. They take me to the store, to the doctor, to the relatives, everywhere . . . I'm just an old man who can't do anything for anyone anymore. I can't even hold my own teacup."

"But . . . but you tell such good stories," said Joshua hopefully.

"Stories? Yes. Stories I have plenty. But you can't eat stories. You can't wear stories. No. Enough stories. I want to do something for your father and mother. But what?" He paused and rubbed his head with a shaking hand. "Maybe I can make them something, as a gift for all their goodness. A gift from me to them. And . . . I think I know exactly what it will be. I think I know. Yes. I already know."

Joshua couldn't wait. "What is it? Uncle Otto? Please? Huh? What?"

"A Hanukkah menorah. I want to make a menorah for them."

"But . . ." Joshua hesitated. Should he say it? Would it make him sad again? "But we . . . we have one already, Uncle Otto."

"Oh, yes, yes. A very nice menorah. Modern. Stream-lined. No decorations. No curves and bends. But I'm going to make a different kind of menorah. In my menorah, the stems for the candles will twist like flowers on a vine, like that menorah I told you about, the menorah of my childhood. When we escaped from Germany, from Hitler, we couldn't take anything. Not our clothes, not our dishes, nothing. Not even my father's menorah. Thank God I was able to come to your parents here in America . . . Yes, I'm going to try to make that menorah come back to life. For your father and mother to give to you someday, and then for you to give to your children someday. That will be my gift. But I need your help. My hands are only good now for waving in the air. These stiff, stupid hands. Will you help me?"

"Yes!" cried Joshua. It was wonderful. Great-Uncle Otto seemed happy again, happier than he'd been for months.

"All right," said Uncle Otto. "Tomorrow. Tomorrow we begin. Tomorrow is menorah day. But remember, it's a secret. It's our secret until the first night of Hanukkah."

JOSHUA RACED home, the snow swirling in streaks like Great-Uncle Otto's thin white hair. He couldn't wait to see his father and mother and *not* tell them the secret, to know something his parents definitely *didn't* know.

"So," said his mother as Joshua stomped his feet and took off his boots. "What have you been doing all afternoon?"

"Nothing."

"Have you been by Uncle Otto's shop?" she asked.

"Uh . . . sure, like always."

"How is he? Did you make him some tea?"

"Sure," said Joshua.

"Why aren't you looking at me? Why are you looking down?" asked his mother. "That means trouble. I can tell every time. What's going on? Is something wrong with Uncle Otto?"

"No, nothing, Mom."

"Hmm. Well, everything comes out in the end," said his mother. "But if you're planning some kind of trick or something, forget it. Remember, Hanukkah is coming, so I have to prepare for all the relatives and I don't have time for your craziness. And don't drive your Uncle Otto crazy either."

Joshua felt as if he would explode with the secret. He started to laugh, but quickly turned the laugh into a cough. It was really hard, harder than he'd ever thought, to keep a secret, *secret*.

The next day, after school, Joshua went directly to Great-Uncle Otto's shop. The sun was out, the snow was melting, and it was yellow-orange autumn again. Uncle Otto was sitting at the window, waiting for him. His face seemed to glow. Joshua almost danced at the sight of his great-uncle looking so eager.

"So, Joshua," Otto said, his voice booming louder than

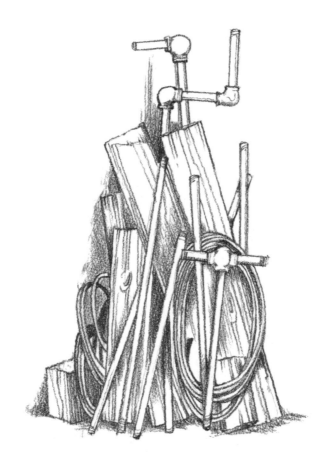

ever, "today is the day we begin. Look, I've cleared a work-table. See all those tubes and wood? That's our menorah."

But it couldn't be. How could those lengths of copper pipe and those blocks of wood ever become a delicate nine-stemmed menorah? It would be easier to turn a stone into a statue.

"Now listen closely," said Great-Uncle Otto. "You have
to become my hands. My fingers. We have to cut this copper
tube with this pipe cutter. You tighten the tube in the vise like
so. Yes, yes. Good, Joshua. And now you pick up the pipe cutter and hold it . . . The other way . . . Yes, good. Now you fit it
in place. Yes. Now turn it. Turn it more . . . Good, good. Very,
very good."

Joshua struggled to hold the tool correctly, the way he'd
seen his great-uncle hold it before he'd become so crippled. But
Joshua's fingers felt unsteady and clumsy, and sometimes his
hand moved one way while the tool moved another. He
worked all afternoon, cutting and filing the tubing into shapes
and sizes to fit the menorah: long tubes to curve outward for
the end candles and straighter tubes toward the center. Little by
little, the tool and his hands began moving smoothly, together.

Every so often, as he worked, Joshua studied his great-
uncle. He looked happy! Happy! No longer sad the way Joshua's dog, Feller, had looked before he'd died.

"Yes! Yes!" said Great-Uncle Otto. "It's beginning to become my father's father's menorah. That beautiful menorah!

. . . What memories! . . . When I was a boy in Europe, we would put it in the window of our old apartment, three flights up. And when it was lit, after the blessings had been said, my cousin and I would run down into the street to see it from below. My father always called 'No,' but we went anyway. We were mischievous, yes. I remember how it was on the eighth night, with all the candles blazing. I would look up at our window, and there was my bird of Ḥanukkah with wings of fire, my beautiful shining Ḥanukkah bird high above that narrow street. I remember, it was so cold my cousin and I had to run back upstairs to all the warm smells and the food and everybody laughing."

"Uncle Otto?" asked Joshua, "was your cousin ever at our house?"

"No . . . no. He didn't come to America. He couldn't escape from Hitler in time. Even your father couldn't help . . . ah, well . . . No sad memories. No . . . In those early days, when we were young, I only saw my cousin once a year, on Ḥanukkah. He lived far away. I remember he and I would be very mischievous sometimes."

"Like me," said Joshua as he filed a copper tube.

"Ah! Worse! Once we took apart an old clock and made dreidels from some of the big gears on their pivots. We didn't know that the clock was still working, was still good. We painted little colored dots on the gears and as we spun them, the dots became circles, one inside the other, blue, green, red, yellow. The next thing I knew, my father was standing there looking at us very sternly. The clock was wrecked. My mother tried to convince him that we had made something just as beautiful and important as the clock. Suddenly I had an idea. I started to spin the clock-dreidels on the table top to show him. And what do you think? After a little while, my father tried spinning one, too. When it jumped off the table, he laughed out loud. Soon, everybody was spinning them, seeing who could make them spin the longest . . . Yes . . . yes . . . We were happy in those old days. But then I grew up. Time passed. And Hitler came with his speeches, his storm troopers, his hate. We were afraid to put a menorah in the window anymore. And soon after that, the real horrors began . . . Well, well . . . Enough.

....

29

Enough stories for today. And enough work for today, too.
All this hard work deserves a rest. Let's have some tea and
crackers.''

Every afternoon that week, Joshua went to the repair
shop to work on the menorah. Great-Uncle Otto selected a

wooden block with a swirling grain and told Joshua how to cut and chisel and drill the block until it became a delicate boat-shaped base to hold the nine copper stems of the menorah in place. And for each stem, Uncle Otto showed him how to fasten a little cup to hold the candle, a cup for every night of Hanukkah.

"So. The first branch is done," said Great-Uncle Otto. "And the second, and the third. See, we have three nights already. It reminds me of something amazing that happened once on the third night of Hanukkah . . . Yes . . ."

"Tell me," said Joshua, as he started to work on the little cup for the fourth candle.

"So long ago . . . as if it happened yesterday. In the old days we were very poor. We lived in one of the oldest parts of the town. The houses were so old that they seemed to lean on each other to hold each other up. Sometimes at night I'd wake up and touch the wall behind my bed to make sure it was still there . . . What was I saying?"

"The third night of Hanukkah," Joshua reminded him.

"Ah, yes. That night, just after the lights had been lit, the

shammes and three more, our apartment started to shake. The plates and cups jumped on the shelves, and some of them shattered on the floor. We thought it was an earthquake. My father took the menorah in one hand and put his free arm around my mother and me, and we all stood in a corner of the room. I felt safe with my father so close. Safe, even though the windows were rattling. Through all this, my father managed to recite the blessings. And suddenly the shaking stopped.

"The next morning, when we looked outside, we saw that the house next door had sunk almost a foot and was pushing right up against our building. It had collapsed from old age, everybody said. But why only *that* house? Nobody really knew. It was so badly damaged, it had to be taken down, stone by stone. For years after, my mother would say that we'd all been spared, everyone, because my father had been so observant, saying the blessings like that. So religious. Yes, I have memories . . . so many special memories . . . "

Slowly, day by day, the menorah on the worktable grew and blossomed like a young tree sending out new branches. And as Joshua worked and listened to the tales of Hanukkahs long past, the menorah in his hands seemed almost to come alive, as if he were holding the very same menorah as the one in the stories.

Yet something was wrong. Great-Uncle Otto shook his head again and again but said nothing. That Friday, during a long afternoon of work, he leaned back and studied the menorah—carefully, with one eye shut.

"It's a good menorah," he said. "A nice menorah. But . . ." He sighed and scratched his chin as he viewed the menorah from the right and then from the left. "But it isn't my father's menorah. Maybe it's all a mistake. Maybe we should stop." The sadness was beginning to appear again in his voice and in his eyes.

"No!" called Joshua. "No! It's a great menorah! Let's try some more! Please?" If they stopped, wouldn't his uncle become like Feller again? And if he became like Feller, wouldn't he die?

"Ah, Joshua. I'm so tired."

"I'll do *everything!* You just tell me! Okay? Okay?" Joshua was surprised at how loud he was shouting. His mother wouldn't call him "the quiet one" now.

"All right. All right. We'll try a little more. Let me think. Maybe—maybe there were more decorations on it. I think there were. We'll have to make some curling vines of copper here and here . . . and here."

Ḥanukkah was drawing closer—four days away, then three, then two—and still Great-Uncle Otto said it wasn't his father's menorah. And with each day, his eyes grew sadder and his body seemed to sag more. Yet at the end of each afternoon, Joshua begged Great-Uncle Otto to try just one more day, one more day. And each afternoon, Otto sighed and said, "Well, well . . . I don't know . . . It's no use."

"Please!"

"All right. All right. One more day."

Finally, on the last day before Ḥanukkah, Otto simply sat and stared out the window, shaking his head again and again.

"Uncle Otto," Joshua called. "Please. Please. Look at what I'm doing. I'm making this tube curve some more. Maybe we still didn't curve the tubes enough." Joshua twisted and turned the copper stems desperately, hoping each new bend would be the right one, the one that would make his great-uncle's face shine like the menorah. Otto just shook his head.

"No. No. It's hopeless," said Great-Uncle Otto. "This isn't my father's menorah. It's hopeless, Joshua, hopeless. Put it on the shelf in the back room. Let it rest. Tomorrow is Hanukkah, and there are no more days, and I'm too tired to work on it anymore. Some other year, some other Hanukkah, maybe we'll try again." Uncle Otto sighed and slumped back in his chair.

Joshua was close to crying. "But . . . but . . . it's beautiful! It's beautiful, no matter what! And we worked so hard! And it was so much fun. And you were so happy making it."

"I know, Joshua, I know. But I wanted to make that menorah come to life again. To give your parents a remembrance of the past. And I can't. Let it sleep on the shelf. Next year maybe. We'll see."

Joshua walked home slowly, downcast and silent. Great-Uncle Otto had looked so old. He seemed to move in slow motion, like Feller had at the end.

THAT NIGHT, the next morning, and all afternoon, the house bustled with his mother's preparations for Hanukkah. And though Joshua helped with the final cleaning, his thoughts were with Great-Uncle Otto sitting in a corner of the living room, staring at something far beyond the walls. Several times Joshua asked if he could get his uncle anything—the newspapers, soda, tea—but each time his uncle shook his head slowly to say no while his hands trembled more than ever. If only there were something he could do. If only, somehow, he could make that menorah become Uncle Otto's father's father's menorah.

Toward evening, Joshua suddenly had an idea. It might work, he thought. It might. But there was hardly any time left. He grabbed his coat and raced out the door to the corner, then ran down the avenue the four long blocks to the repair shop.

At the shop, Joshua jiggled the key the way his great-uncle had shown him, and the big iron door swung open. Quickly he went toward the back of the shop, to the shelf holding the menorah. There it stood in the dim light, a shining crown waiting to be worn.

Joshua stood on a chair, took the menorah from the shelf, and put it carefully on the table. He studied it for a moment, scarcely breathing. Could he do it? Some part of him was fighting desperately against it, against this crazy idea. He'd never done anything like this before, in all his life.

No more thinking! No more! Joshua suddenly pushed the menorah off the worktable. It fell to the floor with a great metallic crash. He felt a streak of pain in his throat. The arms of the menorah were all bent sideways, out of shape. For a second, Joshua felt as if he were the very boy his great-uncle had been so many years ago, standing in dread before the wrecked menorah.

He paused for a moment, hardly breathing. It had to work! Then he started to bend each thin copper tube back into place. He put the menorah on the table from time to time, to examine it the way Great-Uncle Otto had, with one eye closed.

"Not yet," he murmured. "Not yet."

Joshua readjusted two of the arms, then stepped back to study the result, again. Better. Better. He took a sheet of rough sandpaper from the workbench at the front of the shop and rubbed it across the arms of the menorah, then across the wooden base.

Yes. That was good. Now it was an old, bent menorah instead of a brand new one. Now it was a two-hundred-year-old menorah that had been dropped and fixed, and had been used again and again. If only he could work some more. But it was late. His aunts and uncles and cousins must be arriving by now. His mother and father would be furious with him for not being there.

He slipped the menorah into a brown paper bag, then hurried out of the shop, jiggling the key to lock the door. With the bag in his hand, Joshua started to half-run, half-walk toward home. He felt a growing tightness in his chest, as he did when he had to stand up in front of the class and give a report. What would Great-Uncle Otto think? Would it just make him sadder? Had he ruined everything?

As Joshua reached his front door, he could hear voices and laughter overflowing from the living room. His parents would be doubly furious. But it would be worth it if only this helped Uncle Otto.

With his coat still on, Joshua walked past the kitchen and paused. The living room was filled with all his relatives. In a distant corner, he could see Great-Uncle Otto sitting in the same place he'd been all day, alone and lost among the bustle of people. Lost, just like Feller.

"Joshua! Where have you been! You're late!" his mother called. "Take off your coat and hurry. We've all been waiting. It's time to light the candles."

Joshua held up the brown paper bag. "But there's . . . there's a present."

"We'll have time for presents later," said his father.

"But it's from Uncle Otto," said Joshua, pulling the me-

norah from the bag. "It's for you and Mom. Uncle Otto made it for you, just like his old menorah from Europe." He turned toward his great-uncle. "Does it look okay, Uncle Otto? I . . . I tried to fix it so it would be like when you dropped it, and your father straightened it, and all."

He studied his great-uncle anxiously to see if he was looking. But Great-Uncle Otto was staring at Joshua's face rather than at the menorah.

"It's absolutely beautiful," said Joshua's mother.

"Like a real old-fashioned menorah," his aunt added.

"Like an antique," someone else said.

Great-Uncle Otto nodded again and again as his hair floated upward. "Now I see . . . now I see what was missing," he said softly. "So many people, so much love. All the love our menorah had seen over the years. That's what was missing. The love. You've added it, Joshua, for me. We can make things with our hands, yes, but a real menorah we can only make with our hearts. *Now* this is the real menorah, the menorah that can never be broken. Thank you, Joshua, for bringing it back to life."

It wasn't all clear to him, but Joshua felt like leaping into the air. It had worked! Somehow, it had worked!

His father took the menorah and set it down gently on the table. "Otto," he said, "this menorah is a mitzvah, an act of goodness for all of us. This will be our menorah in this family, forever. Thank you for making this beautiful thing."

"I didn't make it. Joshua did. It's his mitzvah, not mine," said Great-Uncle Otto, his voice gathering strength. "But listen, a menorah isn't a menorah until its candles are lit. The menorah is begging for lights!"

Though it was a solemn moment, Joshua couldn't help smiling as he placed the candles in the menorah, for *this* was the great-uncle of the repair shop, the uncle of the booming voice and grandly waving arm.

Joshua took his great-uncle's hand, and helped him to light the center candle of the menorah. Then he carefully gave the *shammes* to his father to light the first candle on the far right. As the blessings were said, the candle flames flickered with every breath.

There was laughter in the room now, and voices, as

Great-Uncle Otto began to sing the old Hanukkah song "Maoz Tsur." All the uncles and aunts joined in, and then the children began singing, too.

Great-Uncle Otto struggled up from his chair, and in the center of the room, crippled and stiff, slowly started to dance. Joshua took one trembling hand while his father took the other, to form a circle with him. And while all three turned slowly to the singing, the flames of the menorah, the old menorah of Europe, nodded and shook and danced with them.

Joshua knew he would remember the happiness in his uncle's face forever. Yes, this would be his own special memory, his own story, the one he would tell *his* children someday: the Hanukkah of his Great-Uncle Otto, whose hair floated as he danced, as if he were light as a bird.

MYRON LEVOY has worked as an engineer on advanced power and propulsion for aerospace, including a proposed manned mission to Mars. Among his books for young readers are *The Witch of Fourth Street and Other Stories*, a Book Week Honor Book, and *Alan and Naomi*, an American Book Award nominee. He and his family live in New Jersey.

DONNA RUFF has taught art and art history in Florida and won an Emmy Award for an animated television piece she did there. Since coming to New York she has illustrated *Our Golda: The Story of Golda Meir*, and numerous book jackets.

X

252584

J   Levoy, Myron
      The Hanukkah of great-
       uncle Otto

DATE		
7 DAYS ONLY		
DURING HOLIDAY SEASON		